The Deepest State

OLIVER WILLIS

ISBN: 9781976996191

DEDICATION

This is dedicated to Paulette Rosemarie Lowe-Willis (1951-2015), my beloved mother who taught me how to read, write, laugh, joke, and appreciate life. Everything good I do, it is thanks to her. The other stuff is me.

CONTENTS

ACKNOWLEDGMENTS

Thanks to everyone on Twitter who liked, shared, and encouraged the original version of this story. You're all sick in the head and I love you for it.

ENTER THE BIDENVERSE

"These goddamn computers are bullshit," Biden growled, trying to enter his password on the laptop, and failing for the third time.

He sat on the porch of his Delaware home next to Dr. Jill Biden, who had heard it all before.

"You need to be more gentle," she reminded him, refusing to look up from her tablet as he raged out.

A vein appeared on Biden's forehead, throbbing in time to his increased heart rate.

The retirement was not sitting well with him. He hated the quiet. The contemplation. No more Senate wheeling and dealing, no more Vice-Presidential jawboning and back-patting.

Sure, he loved the hell out of his beautiful wife. Loved it when the grandkids came over and he got to roll around in the dirt with them, but his bones ached for the glory days.

As the website asked him to remember his first car, Biden's mind wandered back in time.

His hair was darker. Thicker at the temples.

He had less of a paunch, and while he never had a six-pack, the young buck that Jilly fell in love with was no slouch either.

It was 1987, the Senate was in recess, and Biden was knee deep in the jungle muck. Reagan was in the White House, the Boss was on the radio and Joseph Robinette Biden Jr. was doing right by America.

The night before he had parachuted into the Amazon, marking the landing zone with a beacon he'd return to in a few days.

Now he was outside the compound, watching and listening.

The men inside were rough. The worst of the worst. They weren't residents, but instead a scruffy band of right-wing milita brothers who had formed a consortium to take their own piece of the drug trade.

Biden adjusted the tie on his shirt and flexed his bare muscles.

He liked to dress up even when the sweltering, damp, rainforest felt like it would overwhelm him. Years in the Senate – 14 years by this point – had made it a habit. The knot of the tie kept him grounded, centered, reminding him why he was wherever he happened to be at the moment.

A radio crackled inside the ramshackle wooden building on the outer perimeter. The voice was German. Biden recognized the accent. East Germany. He'd been there, under deep cover. He hoped someday soon the wall would fall.

The voice on the other end was relaying drop dates, planned shipments of raw materials for drugs. Those drugs would soon be on American streets.

Biden silently prayed to himself that sooner or later his crime bill would go from pipe dream to law.

He focused back on the present.

He wasn't here for drugs. This mission was personal.

The guard fell as Biden shot two bullets into his spine. The silencer reduced the noise to a soft "thwip" as the body fell to the floor. Biden put his hand over the man's mouth and stared at his wedding ring as he let nature take it's course.

He was in.

Biden hid underneath a shadowy overhang as he stepped along the camp's perimeter.

He ducked down as he walked past an open fire and the seven men huddled around it. They were all beefy, thick, racists out for a quick buck.

"Head in the game," he thought to himself. He had to focus. Not here for the drugs. But he'd deal with them soon.

There, in the warehouse near the middle of the camp. Biden ran over, taking care to keep his feet low to the ground to avoid making any noise. He'd learned a lot at the Academy, where he had been taught all the techniques to kill a man, and to save a man's life.

He pulled himself up to the window and peered in.

The room was dark, with one soft sliver of light that came from the crack in the door hinge.

It was enough.

In the dark, he saw the thick, black hair. The same hair that had testified before Congress in an attempt to stop the Vietnam War, the same hair he saw on the Senate floor, his comrade-in-arms who voted with him.

Kerry.

John Kerry was tied to the chair. His face was red from beatings. Biden knew Kerry hadn't given up any information on the agency. He would rather die than do that.

But the gang would still try. And when they grew tired of his refusal to squeal, they would kill him.

Biden wouldn't let it happen. He was going to save his friend, not as repayment for what happened in Greece, but because it was the right thing to do.

The door creaked slightly as Biden used his device to melt down the lock, reminding himself to buy a fruit basket for those scientist boys and gals who came up with his never-ending supply of gizmos. He didn't have a damned clue how the devices worked, but he knew that most importantly – they did work.

He quickly put a hand on Kerry's shoulder to stir him.

"John, John, God love ya, it's Joe."

Kerry groaned in response, his face swollen from the attacks he had faced.

"God damn, John. Those sons of bitches. Can you walk?"

Kerry slowly nodded his head as Biden loosened his restraints.

Kerry rose from the seat, and Biden slipped his arm underneath his comrade's to steady him.

"I'm getting you the fuck out of here," Biden whispered.

"Good show," Kerry replied, flashing his toothy grin in his friend's direction.

The pair shuffled across the floor, Kerry wincing with each step as the pain shot through his long legs.

Biden wanted to get out of here, quick, but Kerry was in no condition to hustle.

They were outside and moving toward the camp entrance when Biden suddenly pulled Kerry to him, pushing him up against the wall.

He leaned in to his ear.

"Stay," he commanded.

Kerry slumped against the wall, feeling a combination of tension about the moment but also happy to give his body a rest.

Biden reached to his holster and pulled out his handgun. The pearl handle had "Malarkey" etched into it, a souvenir of the Vancouver operation.

He had planted an old twig near the open flame site and had been listening out for its particular sound as a thick East German boot stepped on it. Years ago, Biden had learned the art of Wood Listening from a Native American tribesman who had learned the same technique through family lore and oral tradition.

It would probably save his life on this day.

"Mein gott!" He heard the men yell as they discovered the open door, and he could hear them running in his direction.

Biden raised Malarkey.

One shot. Two shots. Three shots. Four shots.

The men fell, each bullet landing squarely in the center of their skulls.

Biden had come in second in the agency's marksmanship competition for the last seven years. He was a good number two.

Three more left.

Biden grabbed Kerry, leaning his friend against him while trying to take as much of the load off his weary legs as possible.

"Let's bug out, John."

"Capital idea, friend."

Bullets whizzed past their ears as the thugs fired after them. The shots were wild and errant, as the men were unnerved by the accuracy of Biden's precision shots.

Still they ran after the Senatorial pair, hoping to kill them before they escaped into the dense woods.

The three thugs ran into the clearing and stopped.

Kerry and Biden were gone.

There was no sign of them running off into the distance, and as they swept the area left and right with their guns, they couldn't see anything.

"What the hell?" Asked one, in Russian-accented English.

"Fuck," responded another, with a German accent.

What sounded like jungle background noise quickly rose above the still forest.

A loud, whistling noise.

The arrow crushed against the Russian's chest, and went right through him. John Kerry stood next to the tree he had been standing to just moments ago, thankful for his wiry frame and the camouflage lessons he had studiously taken notes through.

The two remaining thugs began to yell but had little time to complete their reverie of terror.

Below them, the jungle mud stirred, and Biden reached out with his calloused hands to grab them by their thighs. He pulled them down, relying on shock and his muscle strength to get them off balance.

As they fell to the ground, he rose from the shallow crevice he had scooped out before entering the camp, thankful that despite his injuries, Kerry's bow skills remained as efficient as ever.

He squeezed two more shots with Malarkey, ending the threat.

"You're a damned animal," Kerry yelled, holding his injured sides as he laughed.

Biden pulled on his aviators and laughed. You don't let friends down, he thought.

"This damned machine is a letdown," he told Jill, even after he had followed her advice and patiently entered his password.

Jill just shook her head. She knew storm clouds were building on the horizon, and despite his complaints, Biden would be called on to go into the field again. She just wanted him to enjoy his downtime, the quiet moments of reflection that were too short and too few in his long life of service.

Finally, the game loaded.

"Biden's going on a Candy Crush!" he announced to anyone within earshot.

THE END

THE DEEPEST STATE

WASHINGTON, DC – STEVE BANNON RESIDENCE
"I'm sorry Steve. But the big boss said it's either him or you. And we can't drop him."

"So now I'm--"

"A total cuck"

"Total?"

"Total. Cuck to the core."

A single tear slid down Steve Bannon's face, streaking the pockmarks on his chin, resting between his two layers of shirts.

WASHINGTON, DC – THE WHITE HOUSE
"Did you do it?"

"Yes, Mr. President"

"Did he cry?"

"Like a choking dog, sir"

"Good. Good. Now, where am I again?"

"The White House, sir."

"Can I have pie?"

"All the pie in the world you want sir.

Donald thought to himself: "I like pie a whole lot, I sure do."

WASHINGTON, DC – THE OBAMA RESIDENCE
"Sir, we just got word."

"Bannon?"

"Yeah. He got cucked."

"Another agent exposed, boss."

"Don't worry, we've got more. Let me be clear: I always have more."

"Hail hydra, sir."

6

"Hail hydra, indeed."

Obama looked at his board and slid a pawn off the surface.

"Always more."

WASHINGTON, DC – THE NAVAL OBSERVATORY

Pence stared at his desk, imagining himself anywhere else but here. There was a knot in his stomach. A sense that at any moment the powder keg could explode. The phone rang. He picked it up.

"You're clear, for now."

"Understood."

His hand shook as he hung up the phone.

"How did I get here?" Pence asked himself.

For God's sake, this was supposed to be a few months on the trail. Some laughs. Now he was deep cover. Nodding along with this idiot. And Obama had him completely compromised. But Mother couldn't know his secret. Never.

Mother knew. She had always known. But she had to play the long game, watching all the boys scurry around like they were the masters of the universe. Mother simply bided her time.

She hated his white hair, though.

WASHINGTON, DC – THE OBAMA RESIDENCE

Michelle Obama rolled her eyes, watching Barack move his chess pieces around. "I love you, but you don't even know." She pulled out her cell phone.

"Situation continues - MO"

"Understood. Everybody gets a car. Everybody. -O"

DELAWARE – THE BIDEN RESIDENCE

"This is bullshit, Jilly. A pile of bullshit," Biden yelled, punching the cold slab of beef that hung from the ceiling in the freezer.

Jill had seen him like this before. Lean. Hungry. Eager. He didn't like being caged like this.

"You have to wait."

"God damn it Jilly."

UTAH – ROMNEY RESIDENCE

"You've got to be joking," Mitt said, admiring his chin in the mirror. It was a great chin.

"No," his son replied.

Mitt wasn't sure which son. But he loved him anyway.

"Bannon, out. Just like the rest."

"Sweet Jehoshaphat, my boy."

WASHINGTON, DC – US CAPITOL

McConnell stood in the dark corner of Ryan's office, running his thin, bony fingers up and down his arms.

"Aren't you cold? Come into the light," Ryan offered.

"I like it here," he replied, "Where I thrive. Dark forces align against us."

"The Dems."

"Indeed, my boy."

CHAPPAQUA, NY – CLINTON RESIDENCE

Bill Clinton walked into the living room, a glass of wine in his left hand, a tablet in the right. He looked over his glasses at Hillary, furiously typing on her keyboard.

"Tweeting?"

"Yes."

"The game is afoot then."

"As always. As always."

WASHINGTON, DC – KUSHNER/TRUMP RESIDENCE

"You have something on your face, Jared." Ivanka reached over with a napkin, rubbing the rough surface against his soft face until it was red.

"I hate how sloppy an eater you are."

"Sorry sweetheart."

"Eat like Daddy does, God damn it."

WASHINGTON, DC – NAVAL OBSERVATORY

"Mother. I have to confess. I had impure thoughts yesterday at 3:15 and at about 6 right before I left the office."

Pence stood in silence, waiting for what always came after the daily report.

Her small hand created a loud crack as it slapped against his jowls.

"Yes, Mother."

WASHINGTON, DC – OBAMA RESIDENCE

Barack held Michelle's hand, his fingers intertwined with hers.

"Do you ever miss it?"

"Some days. Not many," she replied.

She felt guilty. She never lied to him like this. But this was bigger than her, him, and everything before.

Oprah had made her swear a blood oath.

RUSSIA – THE KREMLIN

"Play it again," Vladimir said.

Yuri sighed to himself. Why couldn't Putin operate the damned DVD player himself. You can run Russia but can't master Sony?

He pressed play.

The room filled again with the sound of Trump's voice. Yuri hated this recording.

Vladimir loved it.

CALIFORNIA – THE OPRAH ESTATE

Oprah held the jade skull in the palm of her hand, idly shifting it left and right as she often did while lounging in her "thought cabana."

This had to be precise. It couldn't be haphazard or an afterthought.

"Lightning quick execution, the Harpo way," she thought.

WASHINGTON, DC – THE WHITE HOUSE

"What if I just left?"

"You can't just leave Mr. President, millions are relying on you"

"But they're fucking idiots in trucker hats. Ivanka said so."

"They love you, sir."

Trump felt trapped, caged, terrified.

Melania allowed a small grin to emerge. She loved his pain.

SOMEWHERE IN EUROPE

"This way."

The German pointed toward the narrow stone path between the bushes. John Kerry pulled at the ends of his coat. The wind blew, intensely.

He hadn't been this excited in years, not since the protest days. It was astonishing what was being done.

DELAWARE – BIDEN RESIDENCE

Biden tried to contain his rage. He steadied his hand as he snipped at the edges of the bonsai tree. Jill had purchased it, hoping he would use it to channel his excess energy.

So far, it had been hit or miss.

He missed it. The crowds. Barack. The fight.

"It hurts."

WASHINGTON, DC – MNUCHIN RESIDENCE

Steve Mnuchin rubbed the stack of hundred-dollar bills across the neck of his wife, Louise Linton. She giggled and fondled her brand-new Prada clutch.

"Do you think poors are ever this happy?"

"No, my love. Some of them, perhaps when they dream. But then they wake up."

WASHINGTON, DC – US CAPITOL

McConnell rose.

He moved across the floor of his Senate office, his bones making a slight hiss with each step. The bowl was full. His staffers were good boys and girls, always doing as told.

He put it to his lips, and the liquid burned its way down his throat.

"Good."

SOMEWHERE

Bannon wept.

WASHINGTON, DC – US CAPITOL

Paul Ryan didn't want to disappoint McConnell. He looked down at the parchment, its edges burnt from the bonfire.

He ground his teeth. He did this when he was nervous.

"Where can I find a corpse? At this hour," he mused to himself. "Dagnabit."

WASHINGTON, DC – THE WHITE HOUSE

John Kelly felt all of his 67 years as he walked down the West Wing Colonnade. He hadn't been able, for a moment, to appreciate the splendor, the history, of the building.

"I'm a babysitter. A bad one," he thought. It had been diaper changes and tantrums for months.

WASHINGTON, DC – THE NAVAL OBSERVATORY

Mother nodded.

"Understood. It has to be done, so it'll get done. You have my word."

Mother hung up, using the other, secure phone that Pence didn't know existed. He could be so oblivious.

Mother would be happy to be done with the whole charade. Oprah was worth it.

WASHINGTON, DC – US CAPITOL

Ivanka had nothing but contempt for the senators. As they spoke, she coolly regarded them, imagining how she would humiliate them when it was all over. Her biggest concern was whether she would allow them to live, or just add to the river of blood.

A gushing river.

CHAPPAQUA, NY – THE CLINTON RESIDENCE

Bill offered to help Hillary, but she had refused. He had watched her, over the last four hours, haul pieces of lumber, by herself, into the garage.

Finally, he asked, "What are you doing, dear?"

"William Jefferson Clinton, you have no imagination," she replied, smirking.

WASHINGTON, DC – BELOW THE OBAMA RESIDENCE

"... and so we're in phase two of our info warfare/disruption campaign. And things are going pretty well, Mr. President."

Obama nodded at the officer and dismissed him from the bunker. This was the biggest operation he had been involved in since Bin Laden. He was hopeful.

He was getting too old to play basketball like he used to, but he didn't want to just spend the next three decades at golf either. This was vital. This kept him going, along with Michelle and the girls. And he knew the Deep State needed a strategist.

He was good at that.

SOMEWHERE IN EUROPE

John Kerry scanned the document a fourth time. He translated the French. It checked out.

He looked up to the figure sitting across from him and tried to read her stoic expression.

"This changes it all," Kerry said in a hoarse whisper.

WASHINGTON, DC – THE RUBIO RESIDENCE

Senator Marco Rubio stared at the mirror on his medicine cabinet. He didn't like what he saw looking back.

"Who the fuck are you anymore, Marco? Why the hell did you even come here?"

He thought about the rallies, the debates.

"Jesus Christ, what have I done?"

WASHINGTON, DC – THE WHITE HOUSE

Jared spun around in his desk chair for the thirtieth time. He was so bored. How do all the normies do it? He couldn't call Ivanka, she'd just yell at him again. And Daddy Donald had told him to stop with the phone calls.

"Boreddddd," he said to nobody in particular.

UTAH – THE ROMNEY ESTATE

Mitt liked to ride the horses, it cleared his head. Ann rode alongside him. It was the only time he truly felt free. He had a lot to think about. The evidence was mindboggling. The deeds that had been done were, frankly, satanic.

"I've made a decision," he shouted to Ann.

WASHINGTON, DC

Jared called her anyway.

The phone clicked, and he could hear her perfectly timed breaths on the other end. She said nothing.

"Ivanka, I'm --"

"Bored. Jared, I'm sick of this."

"But it hurts my head so much."

"THIS IS FOR US. I TOLD YOU ITS FOR US. SO SUCK IT UP."

CYBERSPACE

OPEN CHAT SESSION

KellyAnne45: I miss our talks.

VladPutKrem: Same

KellyAnne45: When will it end

VladPutKrem: Stay on task. I believe in you.

KellyAnne45: It isn't the same, not like that summer

VladPutKrem: We always have the tower

KellyAnne45: Promise?

VladPutKrem: Pinky swear

ARKANSAS – REPUBLICAN PARTY DINNER

Grip. Grin. Grip. Grin.

Pence didn't really know where he was anymore. One local Republican club had morphed into another. The faces were all the same, frozen in time. He gave them the same dumb smile, knowing how phony it all was.

Obama had him in a vice, as did Putin.

WASHINGTON – THE TREASURY DEPARTMENT

Mnuchin had become accustomed to the daily flirtations with illegality, but this made him widen his eyes.

"Just like that? But it's drug money."

"Nobody needs to know," Don Jr said, "Dad does this all the time. And we own the DEA now. Your wife likes pretty things, right?"

CALIFORNIA – THE WINFREY MANSION

The man handed Oprah a manila folder. She was old school, liked to feel the information, not just read it on a screen.

"This is good," she cooed, "really good."

"Happy to hear it ma'am."

"How are the boys in R+D dealing with it?"

"Several scenarios, nothing we can't handle."

"Good."

MARYLAND – UNDISCLOSED CEMETARY

Paul Ryan had paid the cemetery groundskeeper in cash to look the other way for a few hours.

His face was flush with sweat as he dug up the dirt, and lamented not having any interns to help him in his ghoulish task.

"Mitch is so weird," he thought as he continued digging.

WASHINGTON, DC

He picked up on the first ring.

"Ivanka?"

"Hello Marco."

Involuntarily, the senator began breathing heavily. She did this to him, and she knew it.

"You can't just call me like this"

"Why not?"

"People will find out."

"Who cares? Daddy owns the CIA, Marco. It's all ours."

SOMEWHERE IN SOUTH AMERICA

They were closing in on Kerry. He could hear their footsteps. A bullet whizzed past his ear.

"Remember your training," the former Secretary of State told himself.

Getting this information back stateside was vital. And only John Forbes Kerry could do it. The others were dead.

CHAPPAQUA, NY – THE CLINTON RESIDENCE

Hillary was done building. Her hands were bloody, a casualty of the splinters from the wood she had been handling. That was okay. This damned thing filled her entire garage. She didn't like hiding from her security detail. But Oprah had called in a favor. So she answered.

WASHINGTON, DC – THE WHITE HOUSE

"Because I'm president!" Trump screamed, droplets of his saliva landing on John Kelly's face.

The former general exhaled, silently, trying not to melt down with Trump. The walls were closing in. Got to keep it together.

"It's just not a good idea sir."

Trump punched him in his mouth.

WASHINGTON, DC – UNDISCLOSED LOCATION

McConnell extended a single, bony finger toward Bannon, shoving it into his chest. The action disrupted the layers of dead skin and salt at the point of contact, kicking up a minuscule cloud of dust.

"You're mine now," McConnell croaked. "Mine."
Bannon nodded, fully cucked.

WASHINGTON, DC – THE WHITE HOUSE
Sarah Sanders hurriedly closed her office door and leaned against it, holding her tablet close to her.
"He looked AT me," she thought.
For months she had tried to get the president's attention. She was beginning to feel invisible. But now he had looked right at her. Maybe.

ATLANTA, GEORGIA – THE CARTER RESIDENCE
Rosalynn Carter nodded along as Jimmy spoke. "He'd kill me if he knew," she thought, staring at the clear, blue Georgia sky. Jimmy didn't notice, he was still deeply, madly in love with her, after all these years.
"Oprah's plan will work," she thought, "It has to."

MANHATTAN, NY – TRUMP TOWER
Eric Trump was so confused as the blood streamed down his forehead, a crimson stamp against his pale, gothic flesh. How had this mysterious force field just appeared in front of his Trump Tower balcony door? Why did it hurt so badly? Where was Daddy, why wouldn't he come home?

WASHINGTON, DC – THE WHITE HOUSE
"You're hurting me."
Pence loosened his grip on Jared's shoulder. The boy was soft.
"Do you understand?"
"I think so."
"Don't 'think' boy. Do."
"Daddy Donald will be mad."
"Do you think I don't know that?"
"Yes sir."
"You do as told. This comes from high up."
"You mean?"
"Yes."

WASHINGTON, DC – RYAN RESIDENCE
"Here I am, using a meat tenderizer on a corpse, heck-a-doodle," Paul Ryan thought as he slammed metal against dead flesh another time.
The body was fresh, and the formaldehyde splashed in his face, the liquid soaking into his widow's peak.
"I hope Mitch is right."

WASHINGTON, DC – UNDISCLOSED LOCATION

Mother held the martini glass loosely, her well-manicured fingers just barely holding on to the glass. Pence thought she was at prayer group.

Oprah nodded in her direction as she directed her gaze across the room. Michelle Obama got a nod too.

Oprah put her hands together.

CHAPPAQUA/ WASHINGTON, DC

"Barack, I just feel like something's up," Bill said, the phone cradled in the corner of his neck. He liked a landline still.

"I mean, maybe," the former President replied.

"Hillary's building shit in the garage"

"Michelle's been quiet lately. Too quiet."

"Somethings up, man."

WASHINGTON, DC – US CAPITOL

Rubio took a big step backwards as he saw the shock of blonde hair emerge from the corner of his office.

"My God, Kellyanne. What the hell are you doing here?"

"You're sloppy, Marco. So damned sloppy."

"What do you mean?"

He nervously slicked his hair back.

"Ivanka."

SOMEWHERE IN SOUTH AMERICA

"I took a life," Kerry thought as he wiped the blood from his hands.

He pulled back on the controls and the helicopter lurched from its spot in the grassy clearing.

This was not what he had signed up for. He was retired. Out of it. And yet, John Kerry was in the fight again.

CALIFORNIA – A STEAK HOUSE

The steak squished as Donald Jr chewed. It was rare, almost still alive. How he loved it. Tiffany wrinkled her nose in disgust. She loathed him. He always hated her.

"How's tricks?"

"You are filth. What you've done is filth."

"Dad says I'm number one killer"

"He would. Filth."

RUSSIA – THE KREMLIN

"There are so many loose ends, President Putin"

Vladimir replied with a dismissive wave. Yuri was always such a worrywart.

"The game will proceed. They all dance for me."
"What of the TV host?"
"The Oprah? She is of no concern. She is a woman, Yuri. We have dealt with the women."

WASHINGTON, DC – UNDISCLOSED LOCATION

Bannon wanted to cry as McConnell spoke, his icy breath chilling the corpulent executive down to his spine. His pimples shriveled in response. But his face remained still. McConnell explained the procedure in detail. Ryan was going to do that? For power?

"Sick," Bannon said.

WASHINGTON, DC – THE MNUCHIN RESIDENCE

Mnuchin couldn't believe it. He clicked "reload," but the bank account said the same thing this time too. Louise would kill him. The furs. The purses.

"I'll have to sell the villa," he realized.

Don Jr had set him up. The cartel had struck. It was all gone.

WASHINGTON, DC – UNDISCLOSED LOCATION

Michelle raised her hand.
Oprah pointed to her, giving her the floor.
"It's magnificent, Ope, it's so bold. But the downside is enormous."
"I understand. I'm asking you all to take a risk here. I get it."
"So you see--"
"Hillary is in."
Michelle raised an eyebrow. So did Mother.
Barbara Bush's pearl necklace glared in the light of the meeting room.
"Hillary?"
Oprah nodded.
"Despite everything? Despite the incident?"
"She said it was in the past, so its in the past. It's time for us to unify."
Barbara held the prime pearl between her fingers.
"Okay."

WASHINGTON, DC – THE KUSHNER/TRUMP RESIDENCE

The water filling the tub was scalding hot. A thick film from the steam covered the full-body mirrors in the Kushner-Trump mansion.

Ivanka lazily put her hand in the water.
She felt nothing.
"Good," she whispered. "I don't want to."
It would be weak, she thought. Weak like Jared.

IN THE AIR OVER THE U.S./MEXICO BORDER

Kerry took a deep breath. The coast was clear. The helicopter shuddered as he flew due west. He grabbed his satellite phone and punched in the number.

"Biden."

"It's John. We need to meet."

"Alpha or Omega?"

"Delta. Delta Six Seven Niner."

"Holy fuck, Kerry."

WASHINGTON, DC – THE WHITE HOUSE

"Mr. President, we can't just nuke them. We have to be strategic."

"Scramble the F-52s then, show them we mean business, they can't mock me this way." Trump thumped the desk with his fist, bruising the underside of his delicate hand.

"Those aren't real planes. They're from a video game."

"Why won't you let me do anything, Kelly? Reince would. Jesus."

WASHINGTON, DC – LAW FIRM

Reince sat at his desk at the law firm. For a moment, he soaked in the quiet, the still. The smell of the ink from the printer wafted into his nostrils and comforted his mind.

He never had to see those stubby fingers again. Never had to be beaten like a piñata. He felt calm.

WASHINGTON, DC – OUTSIDE THE OBAMA RESIDENCE

"Mr. President, checking in"

"Morning, Comey"

Obama liked to get the calls out of the way during his morning run.

"We've executed the protocol as you laid out. Ivanka is on the wire, but we believe she is completely in the dark."

"Perfect. That's great. Just great, Jim."

WASHINGTON, DC – THE KUSHNER/TRUMP RESIDENCE

Jared sat in the bathroom, fully clothed, on top of the toilet. He could feel the thin filament from the recording device brushing against his neck. What if she found it? Shed kill him for sure. Really kill him. Shed told him about Eric and the homeless man. It had been a threat.

WASHINGTON, DC – IN TRANSIT

The car was silent as Michelle hung up from the girls. They were the reason she had gone to these lengths, why she was back in the game up to her eyeballs, despite her hatred of Washington.

"Terrorist fist jab," she ruefully chuckled. "Damn 'em."

UTAH/ WASHINGTON, DC

"Marco, this line is for emergencies only, for heaven's sake"

"Sweet Jesus, Mitt, they know about us"

"The Ivanka thing?"

"Yes."

"Holy Toledo with a squeeze of lemon. I told you: Be discreet."

"We tried... But I'm weak."

"Buck up, chum. We'll noodle this one through."

WASHINGTON, DC – THE RYAN RESIDENCE

Paul Ryan stared at the square of meat.

"Jiminy Christmas, I just don't know."

It jiggled when he touched it, the gelatinous mass inside reacting to his index finger.

"Mitch sure has some wacky ideas. But if this beastly fellah helps him, why not me, huh? Worth a shot."

CALIFORNIA/CHAPPAQUA, NY

"It's a go," Oprah said.

Hillary nodded in the affirmative over the video feed.

"Everyone? Even Michelle and Barbara?"

"Both of them. Mother too."

"I expected her. She's always been with us."

"My Prague contact said Kerry made it out."

"I'm glad. He's good people."

WYOMING

Cheney floated in a vat filled with clear oil, a custom mix he'd picked up outside of Baghdad from a Romanian arms dealer. The old-fashioned speaker hanging from the ceiling of his private sanctum squawked to life.

"Kerry escaped"

Cheney snarled, a small bubble forming on his lip.

KENNEBUNKPORT, MAINE – BUSH FAMILY COMPOUND

"Heavens mother, you gave me a fright"

"Calm down, Jeb."

Barbara Bush continued to fiddle with her pearls, it was a nervous tic she'd picked up in George's term.

"There are some... things coming, Jeb. And I want you to move your money into the gold bars. Just in case."

"Yes, mother."

MANHATTAN, NY – TRUMP TOWER
Eric Trump laid in his custom coffin, took a pull from his juice box and mumbled "I'm a vampire, grrrrrr."

WASHINGTON, DC – THE KUSHNER/TRUMP RESIDENCE
Ivanka cut her peanut butter and jelly sandwich into 24 individual squares, like always, and chewed each bit 32 times.

Jared's cutlery clinked against the crystal glass, half filled with water.

He was in a cold sweat.

"What?"

"Sorry, love. I may have the sniffles."

"Ew."

WASHINGTON, DC – CONWAY RESIDENCE
Kellyanne loved to recline on her silk-covered chaise lounge while shooting her handgun at the Democratic donkey targets she had picked up at the NRA convention.

On the phone, Vladimir was muttering.

"Shh," she instructed him.

"What, my rose?"

"I caught Marco. Photos and all."

DELAWARE – BIDEN RESIDENCE
Biden walked up to the helicopter as the blades were still softly spinning. He grabbed Kerry in an enormous bear hug.

"Jesus Christ, my man"

"Indeed, friend. I have seen some shit."

"Bet you have. Bet you have. C'mon, I got some beers and brats on the grill. Unload."

CALIFORNIA – WINFREY MANSION
Oprah leaned back, and the recliner shot into the air, quickly at first, slowing down when it hit the top of its path. The data was projected on to the giant inside surface of the sphere. She checked her math. Solid. She slid her finger onto the plate with the thumbprint scanner.

WASHINGTON, DC – RYAN RESIDENCE
The room smelled of dead flesh.

Paul Ryan held his chin, then read the incantation. This all felt strange and uncomfortable. "Here goes."

He swallowed the cube of body meat, whole.

He repeated the unholy words.

19

He closed his eyes and held them shut.
Across town, Mitch stirred.

WASHINGTON, DC – THE WHITE HOUSE
Melania had built up a wall of pillows between them, but she still stared up at the ceiling, sensing his presence in the bed next to her. In his sleep, he mumbled racial epithets. She cursed him and dreamed of the old country.

CALIFORNIA – A STEAK HOUSE
Don Jr walked away from Tiffany, who glared at him with such intensity he could almost feel it at the ends of his heavily-greased hairs. He did the tough guy thing with her, but deep inside, he wanted a sister. At least she would talk to him. Ivanka said nothing.

CALIFORNIA – WINFREY MANSION
"Condition alpha has been achieved," Oprah relayed to the array of nodes that had come alive on her spherical info-screen. She continued to hold the jade skull, sensing history focusing on this point, at this moment. "Find your truths," she commanded.
In response, they saluted.

CHAPPAQUA, NEW YORK – CLINTON RESIDENCE
As she finished her salute, Hillary reached over and turned off her workstation. In the next room, Bill slept soundly, doing that soft purr he always did when in deepest of sleeps.
She strapped on her leather gloves, ready to work.

ATLANTA, GEORGIA – CARTER RESIDENCE
Jimmy Carter slept soundly as well. Rosalynn was already out in the garden. The storm was coming, but her flowers would not be neglected.

WASHINGTON, DC – OBAMA RESIDENCE
Michelle swung her leg in a furious roundhouse kick, connecting with the head of the practice dummy. It made a loud CRACK and went skittering across the floor of her dojo.
"Have to buy a new one," she thought, turning to the exit.

RUSSIA – THE KREMLIN
Yuri listened to the report, nodding as the details were read off to him. They were small things, anomalies maybe. Nothing earth shattering. At first glance.
He considered alerting Putin.
"Better not, he'll bite my head off," he decided.

WASHINGTON – RYAN RESIDENCE
"Heck!" Paul Ryan yelped. "Heck! Gosh! Golly!" He continued.

Gasses bubbled. A cat howled. His skin grew warm.

A spiderweb-shaped red pattern began to emerge at the base of his neck. It crawled up, covering his mouth, tugging at his lips.

He could see. Mitch.

UTAH – ROMNEY RESIDENCE
Mitt pulled the lever and the finely tuned gears leapt into action, lowering the car elevator deep into the earth.

He put an arm around Rubio.

"We'll get you squared away, chum. We've got tricks those she-devils don't know"

Rubio gulped.

"Wowsers, Mitt," he replied.

SOMEWHERE BELOW WASHINGTON, DC
Bannon's fingers bled as he tugged at the coal fragments. He was more husk than man now, moving in stiff, zombie-like motions. He could only helplessly watch as his body acted beyond his control.

Mitch sat in the cool, dark as always.

The hairs on his neck stood up.

"Ryan."

DELAWARE – BIDEN RESIDENCE
Biden pulled the exquisitely polished wooden cabinet open and gestured to the array of weapons inside.

Kerry's eyes widened.

Biden grinned.

"That's right you sonofabitch. Barack loaded me up. The best shit."

"This is the real deal, friend."

Biden guffawed and slapped his shoulders.

WASHINGTON, DC – NAVAL OBSERVATORY
Mother walked towards Pence.

"Dear. Headed out?"

"Doing some shopping"

"Have fun"

She gave him a slight nod and continued on. She felt the weight of the switchblade in her coat pocket.

If he doesn't want to see, he won't.

WASHINGTON, DC – MNUCHIN RESIDENCE

Louise Linton wrinkled her nose in confusion. Mnuchin pushed his horn-rimmed glasses up on his nose as they slid on his slick sweat.

"What do you mean the money is gone?"

"It -- is."

"But my things, my precious things."

"The cartel won't take no for an answer, Louise."

DALLAS, TEXAS – BUSH RESIDENCE

When George W. Bush painted, he wouldn't hear the screams. He spent the days fueled on caffeine to fend off the night terrors.

He wasn't sure what was real and what was imaginary.

Laura turned into a dragon.

Bring 'er on.

SOMEWHERE

Blood sprayed as the throat was slit. The agent didn't give it a second thought. His devotion to Oprah was supreme. Her commands were his mandate.

Oprah or death was his creed.

WASHINGTON, DC/OTTAWA

"Trudeau."

"Justin. It's Obama."

"Barack! So good to hear from you."

"Same. Look, Biden is off grid again. My operation needs some eyes in the air."

"It's yours," he said, slathering on the poutine.

It felt like old days, before the change.

MANHATTAN, NY – TRUMP TOWER

Human flesh is gummier than you'd think, Eric thought.

UNDISCLOSED LOCATION

Ivanka interrupted Bolivar mid-rant.

"There's no reason to buy so much ammunition. We just need a few feet of rope to make enough garrotes to wipe out the Duhane Cartel's operation. I've run the numbers."

The cocaine baron was impressed.

WASHINGTON, DC – THE WHITE HOUSE

Pence nodded, his nervous tick going into overdrive as Vladimir Putin reeled off a series of instructions over the phone.

He tried to memorize all of it - he couldn't leave a paper trail of course -

but he worried about forgetting a step.

His hands shook.

WYOMING – CHENEY RESIDENCE

Looking at the rifles, Cheney made a sour smile and remembered how he had shot his friend.

That was a simpler time. You just wound up idiot George and he would go. Now, Cheney had to get his hands dirty. If you wanted a South American revolution you had to do it yourself.

WASHINGTON, DC – RYAN RESIDENCE

"What in tarnation am I seeing?" Paul Ryan wondered.

Everything was in a red haze. He felt separated from his body, like he was watching a film back at the movie house in Janesville.

"I can taste the colors," he realized.

How did Mitch live like this?

THE ARCTIC REGION

"Joe. Enough."

"No, John, this joker's got to see what a bunch of malarkey this is for fuck's sake"

Biden tightened his grip on the ivory handle of his blade, nicknamed M'Lady, and twisted it wickedly.

The man screamed in agony.

Kerry wondered if they'd crossed a line.

WASHINGTON, DC/CHAPPAQUA, NY

"Bill. I cannot do it anymore. He's gotten worse. He's somehow more cruel, more deranged."

"Melania, dear, I understand. And I know how hard this has been, but you must gather more evidence for The Brotherhood."

"You promised safe passage for me and my boy."

"I still do."

UTAH – BELOW THE ROMNEY ESTATE

Mitt hated feeling this judgmental, but he hated how impulsive men like Marco were. He had been able to keep himself in check for decades, denying vice and temptation.

But these men -- boys really -- like Marco and Jared, they were so soft.

"Phooey," Mitt thought.

SOMEWHERE

Hillary gunned the engine, aiming the car directly at the ravine. Michelle leaned out the passenger window, an Uzi in each hand.

The sound of gunfire was deafening.

All of their past tension, strife, disagreement was gone, replaced with a harmonious ballet of righteous violence.

ROCK CREEK PARK, WASHINGTON, DC

Bannon galloped on all fours, rushing through the thick grass that slashed against his bare skin. He would feel pain in the morning but now he was a soulless beast of burden.

Mitch, his rider, squeezed his bony knees against him, prodding him to run faster.

"Make haste, boy."

MANHATTAN, NY – TRUMP TOWER

Don Jr winced as he held the severed goat's head. He hated doing this. It should have been someone else's job. But Daddy had tasked him as Eric's overseer decades ago.

He watched his brother scratch against the walls.

He had gone feral again, and needed feeding.

CALIFORNIA – WINFREY RESIDENCE

Steadman Graham softly caressed Oprah's shoulders and quietly whispered, "Is it everything you dreamed?"

"Yes," she replied, "my spirit soars."

They watched together as the satellite feeds showed multiple scenes of extreme violence, done in her name.

"More wine?"

SOMEWHERE

Mother felt uncaged. After years at Pence's side, keeping her animal instincts at bay, playing her deep cover role as the good wife -- that wasn't her true self.

This was.

She leapt from the tree.

Her kitana blade shone in the moonlight.

Her prey's death was quick.

BERLIN, GERMANY

Angela Merkel liked her scotch neat, and that's how Fritz made it.

She sat in her leather command chair, it's sweet musk reminding her of life on Papa's farm.

Fritz couldn't understand all of it. He saw the pieces, but it was bewildering. Angela understood. She stroked her chin.

WASHINGTON, DC – BELOW THE OBAMA RESIDENCE
Miles below Washington DC, a map of the world on a gigantic wall screen was lit up with red incident alerts in multiple cities.

"I'm such an idiot." Obama said to nobody in particular. "Right under my nose. In my own bed. And I was completely clueless."

WASHINGTON, DC – THE WHITE HOUSE
Trump looked on stupidly as Ivanka and John Kelly spoke in terse, clipped sentences.

She was still in her silk pajamas, assembled by a host of 10-year-olds the day she visited the factory in China.

Trump didn't understand any of what they were saying, but she was mad.

UTAH – BELOW THE ROMNEY RESIDENCE
Rubio nodded, watching Mitt's hands as he showed him how to mix the elixir.

Involuntarily, he began to lick his lips. He was nervous. He felt like it was Chris Christie mocking him again.

"Sport, I need you present," Mitt said, "Your first kill is always your hardest."

WASHINGTON, DC – THE WHITE HOUSE
"But she's black," Ivanka said through gritted teeth. She spoke in her signature monotone - thank you finishing school - but her clenched fists betrayed her deep and unyielding anger.

John Kelly stared at the floor.

"Oprah is a black," Ivanka continued, trying to comprehend it.

MANHATTAN, NY – TRUMP TOWER
Eric shat on the floor in the corner of his enclosure, oblivious to the world.

SOMEWHERE
Hillary radioed headquarters and filled them in that another facility had been secured.

The walls inside still dripped with blood.

Michelle leaned against the candy apple red Mustang, watching the flames lick the sky.

ROCK CREEK PARK – WASHINGTON, DC
Pence glared at the Secret Service agent. He backed off, stationing himself at the entrance to the woods.

Pence's cover story was prayer and quiet contemplation. That was the only way to shake his detail.

"Vladimir sent me."

"I know," said Boris Johnson, "Me too."

WASHINGTON, DC – RYAN RESIDENCE

McConnell dismounted Bannon and left him to lick his wounds.

He soon found Ryan, his earth-bound body convulsing amidst copies of The Fountainhead. "The gods are displeased," he hissed with his forked tongue.

CHAPPAQUA, NY – CLINTON RESIDENCE

Bill chuckled as he hung up the phone. The caller had confirmed what he already knew: The network was done, smashed beyond repair. Much of the wet work had been done by Hillary and Michelle.

"Oh dear," he whispered, knowing what this could mean.

"Oprah has the upper hand."

SOMEWHERE IN THE ARCTIC

The cold tugged at the corners of Biden's eyes. Waves of snow fell, blocking his view of the path ahead. He sniffed the air, straining to catch some familiar scent.

"Anything?" Kerry asked from behind him.

"No," he growled.

Kerry slowly nodded.

WASHINGTON, DC – WHITE HOUSE

Kellyanne hung upside down, supported only by her knees wrapped around the tension bar. With each crunch, she felt tension in her abdomen.

The network she had known her entire life was wiped out.

She would adapt. She always did.

"Feel the burn," she grunted.

WASHINGTON, DC – THE KUSHNER/TRUMP RESIDENCE

Ivanka pulled in close to Jared. Her lips almost touched his ear, but not quite. He could feel her breath as she spoke. Somehow it was cold, not warm.

"You betrayed our family. I will end you. I promise."

Jared began shaking.

SOUTH AMERICA – CARTEL MANSION

Don Jr stared at the centerpiece, afraid to look away. He could hear the bonfire crackling behind him. He puckered his lips.

This had been a bad idea. He loved the cartel's money, but now he was at a party surrounded by brown-skinned people. He feared them. So much.

SAN DIEGO, CALIFORNIA – ARBY'S

Tiffany Trump made her way to the booth in the back of the Arby's. Her dining partner bit his way into his roast beef sandwich, trying as best he could to stay inconspicuous. It was impossible. He was too tall.

"Director Comey"

"Tiffany! It's just Jim," he replied.

CALIFORNIA – WINFREY MANSION

Oprah dismissed Steadman from the thought cabana and dipped her fingers into the man-made confidence stream that wound its way through the building. She let her pride have a moment of reflection. Any complications seemed far off and nearly impossible to fathom.

WASHINGTON/UNDISCLOSED LOCATION VIA SATELLITE PHONE

She picked up.

"Barack"

"Michelle"

"I'm sorry, I just"

"I know. You did what you had to"

"All these years, how did u do it?"

"It wasn't easy. Especially lying to you"

"I know"

"What's done is done. Let me be clear."

She smiled.

WASHINGTON, DC

After the exchange, Boris Johnson walked back towards the embassy, his head hung low. Not only was he betraying his queen, but also, he was simply an errand boy for the Russian.

From Buckingham Palace, the queen watched him via drone, disgusted.

SANCTUM MCCONNELL

McConnell hoisted Paul Ryan's body onto the altar. It twitched and convulsed as it had for the last few hours.

McConnell emitted a resigned sigh that echoed through his hollow gullet.

He had tried to warn his apprentice. Now he was trapped between realms.

The blood ritual began.

WASHINGTON, DC – THE WHITE HOUSE
The frosting was all over Trump's face. He had dug into the smash cake with his two diminutive hands, wrecking the "45" the White House bakers had stenciled into the middle.

John Kelly tried to smile but continued to die inside. This disaster never ended.

"My cake!" Trump yelled

CALIFORNIA – WINFREY RESIDENCE
Obama sat across from Oprah.

"I won't lie. I admire what you've done here. In many ways, it surpasses our own efforts."

"We tried. I hope you can get past the deception."

"One needs discretion when playing the grand game. I understand it."

"Can we work together now?"

WASHINGTON, DC – THE NAVAL OBSERVATORY
Mother crossed her legs and sipped her tea, listening to Pence. Her role, as always, was to listen and nod silently. In her mind, she relived the last few days, in the jungles, hearing the screams and howls as she truly lived.

She nodded, as he went on in excruciating detail.

SOMEWHERE
The potato sack was pulled off Jared's head. The light blinded him. His face and hair were drenched with sweat. He was disoriented. His hands bound.

Ivanka walked to him, her arms folded.

"Who set you up with a wire? Who did this?"

Her eyes narrowed.

LONDON, ENGLAND – BUCKINGHAM PALACE
"First Brexit, now this," the Queen said, gesturing to the photos of Boris Johnson exchanging the suitcase with Pence. "I've a good mind to change things around here. Back to the old days, Brittania and all of that."

Theresa May gulped. "Ma'am --"

"Shut up. One has had enough."

SOMEWHERE IN THE ARCTIC
Biden's muscles strained as he pulled Kerry up to the landing.

"Thanks, friend"

"Can't go all this way and lose the sonofabitch that's got my back"

Kerry gave him a wry smile. They'd traveled far. The final destination was now feet away. He checked his gun.

WASHINGTON, DC – THE WHITE HOUSE

Sarah Sanders listened to the NBC reporter's question and casually let her pinkie finger brush against the trap door button. She felt an electric thrill slide up her spine and nodded "no" to yet another question. One day she would press it, and make their nightmares come to life.

CHAPPAQUA, NEW YORK

Hillary and Michelle hugged. Theirs was a bond now forged in fire. They had watched each other's backs, fought – and even killed for a great cause. They were forever connected.

"Oprah."

"Oprah."

Hillary walked towards her home as Michelle pulled off in her muscle car.

SOMEWHERE

The head of the cartel looked away. He had seen unmentionable brutality, but this was... beyond.

Ivanka screamed in primal rage as she let him have it.

Jared began to tell them everything.

"I knew you'd break," she whispered as she spat onto the ground next to his bare feet.

CALIFORNIA – ARBY'S

Comey sighed, assessing the entire sordid saga Tiffany had laid out for him. He had kept notes as she spoke. Three single-spaced handwritten pages. The crimes were local, state, federal, international.

"Your brother is in trouble."

"Don't call him that. He's just a boy I know."

WASHINGTON, DC – RUBIO RESIDENCE

Rubio found himself staring at Kellyanne's bicep.

He nervously laughed.

He could hear Romney in his head, coaching him through.

He wasn't sure if he could go through with it. His stomach churned.

"More wine?"

"Get to the point, Marco. I'm a busy woman. I work for the president."

"You have toyed with magicks beyond your comprehension," McConnell hissed as his spirit form appeared across from Ryan's on the ethereal plane.

"Boy howdy," he replied, "I just wanted some darn tax cuts."

"Foolish mortal."

"Quite a pickle, Mitch."

SOMEWHERE IN THE ARCTIC CIRCLE

Biden arched his back but was only able to separate a few inches from Kerry, whose back was tied to his.

"It's like Rangoon all over again," Biden yelled, blood on his gleaming white teeth.

He felt a vibration as Kerry chuckled. The black eye hadn't killed his sense of humor.

MANHATTAN, NY – TRUMP TOWER

The toy had been designed to entertain cats. The end of it was a tail that flicked to-and-fro. Eric could not figure it out, and for the last two hours it had completely consumed his attention.

Cheney emerged from the shack, his fists encased in solid gold gloves. He looked at Biden and Kerry, unbowed, tied to each other.

He opened one end of his mouth and a cackle emerged, the sound of metal clanging from Cheney's body accompanying it.

"You both think you're so smart."

RUSSIA – THE KREMLIN

Yuri walked in the direction of the throne room, taking his time.

He was in no rush.

Inside, Putin sat in the middle of his tantrum's aftermath.

Paintings ripped. Furniture cut up.

He was beyond livid.

Yuri's slick hand slipped off the door handle, delaying the inevitable.

CHAPPAQUA, NEW YORK/SOMEWHERE ELSE

Hillary opened the door.

Bill wasn't there. It was unusual for him to be gone like this.

Obama looked at Bill.

Both men gripped their guns and looked down.

Sparks spewed from Cheney's golden manacles.

WASHINGTON, DC – THE KUSHNER/TRUMP RESIDENCE

Ivanka seethed with rage. She had foolishly believed she had excised all feelings, but Jared's betrayal had brought them back to life.

Daddy was vulnerable.

Oprah and Putin circled like vultures.

"I can play too," she told the cartel.

SANCTUM MCCONNELL
Black gas belched from Ryan's eyes, mouth and nose. McConnell considered simply abandoning him. He had trifled with the darkest magick.

One last try, as payment for backing tax cuts.

McConnell spoke in tongues.

The demons howled.

SOMEWHERE IN THE ARCTIC CIRCLE
Bill Clinton felt 20 years younger, his fists wet with blood, his heart pumping. Obama had done his thing, deftly jumping over bodies, neutralizing the enemy without batting an eye. Bill was more like a bull in a China shop than Obama's graceful gazelle. But the job was done.

RUSSIA – THE KREMLIN
Putin was still angry. The incompetence was staggering. His operation was in retreat, and they hadn't seen it coming.

His phone rang. Not the red one. The one next to it. A bright yellow light flashed.

He picked up.

"This is Oprah."

SOMEWHERE IN THE ARCTIC CIRCLE
"Joe."

"Barack."

The old friends regarded each other as Obama loosened his restraints. In the corner, a shell-shocked Cheney moaned. His golden manacles shattered after Clinton's deployment of the sonic weapon.

"I knew you'd show"

"I cut it close"

"You guys," Kerry chuckled.

WASHINGTON, DC – THE RUBIO RESIDENCE
Rubio poured the vial.

Kellyanne was busy retelling how she had left a CNN host tongue-tied.

The liquid bubbled and hissed.

Rubio considered flip-flopping as he so often did, throwing out the concoction. "No, do it," he steeled himself.

CLINTON RESIDENCE / THE ARCTIC CIRCLE
"Dear"

Hillary rolled her eyes at the sound of Bill's voice.

"You're out with Biden again"

"Yes --"

"Bill."

"But Obama's here too. Kerry also."

She felt better hearing that. He and Biden were a train wreck together. Obama was on point, however.

WASHINGTON, DC – THE RUBIO RESIDENCE

Kellyanne downed her drink in one gulp. Rubio arched his eyebrow, anticipating... something.

She laughed.

"Oh, Marco. You and Mitt thought I'd drink your little tea and just collapse at your feet. We who serve the dark forces are immune to your earth poisons."

SOMEWHERE IN THE ARCTIC CIRCLE

Cheney snarled as Kerry tied him down on the backseat of the helicopter.

"Behave!" Biden commanded, and rapped him on the nose with a newspaper.

He turned to Obama and embraced him. "Good workin' with you again, chief."

"Same."

The Hague would have a new prisoner, soon.

RUSSIA – THE KREMLIN

The Kremlin was in darkness. Putin stared at his display. It was chaos. All his pieces were in disarray. He could still hear Oprah's voice, echoing over the phone. That laugh. She had him over a barrel. It wasn't over. But he was no longer on top.

WASHINGTON, DC – KUSHNER/TRUMP RESIDENCE

She kept Jared close to her. She could have punished him further, but she preferred to prolong his humiliation. Ivanka pressed a button, and the screen in the middle of the desk lit up with a map.

"This is how we get back in the game," she began.

Jared stared at the ground.

LONDON, ENGLAND – JOHNSON RESIDENCE

Boris Johnson stepped out of the shower and dried his hair. He tried to recreate his signature "unkempt" look. The smoke grenade landed next to his feet. In seconds he was nose to nose with James Corden.

"The Queen wants a word, you Russian stooge."

Johnson fell to his knees.

WASHINGTON, DC – MCCONNELL RESIDENCE, EARTH PLANE

Paul Ryan woke up with a scream. He felt like he had been screaming for days. McConnell pulled away the sopping wet palm fronds that covered his body and slithered next to Ryan.

"You live"

"I've seen the other side. How did you..."

"Rest, boy. We have work to do."

MANHATTAN, NY – TRUMP TOWER

Eric Trump could not figure out how to get his straw into the box of apple juice and began to cry.

SOMEWHERE IN MIDDLE AMERICA

Comey nodded. This was a long strange, trip. He felt he was on the right side of history, but he thought about the costs and the damage that had been inflicted.

On his screen, Oprah nodded and cut off the transmission.

This was for the best, Comey thought. Wasn't it?

WASHINGTON, D.C. – THE WHITE HOUSE

Tiffany had her arms crossed across her chest. Her father sat at his desk in the Oval Office, scowling.

"So great, Tiff."

At least he remembered my name, she thought.

"This isn't for you... Dad." She spat out the last word.

"Tiffany, come on."

"I didn't like lying to Comey."

WASHINGTON, D.C. – THE RUBIO RESIDENCE

A dark, black cloud enveloped Marco Rubio.

SOMEWHERE SOUTH OF THE BORDER

Donald Jr practiced his "tough guy" face in the bathroom mirror. He liked to use it with the cartel because they felt so brown, so tough. The money was in the account. He wanted to run. But this was about his father. They had to fight back.

CALIFORNIA – THE OPRAH ESTATE

Hillary had one knee down on the exquisite Italian tile. She rested on her old sword, it's steel gleaming in the tasteful lighting, the smell of fall wafting through the breezeway. Outside, light rain drops fell against the thick glass windows.

"Rise," said Oprah.

"We have a lot of work to do," Oprah said. Hillary nodded. "This first strike reset the chess board. But the others - Putin, Trump - won't sit still."

"They never do," Hillary answered.

"We have to be prepared."

"We will be."

WASHINGTON, DC – THE OBAMA RESIDENCE

Barack Obama smiled. Michelle smiled back.

"It's quiet," he noted.

"It's never quiet, Barack. The whole game is back."

"I know. I know. You should have just told me."

"You boys can't keep a secret."

"True."

- END EPISODE I –

POST-CREDIT SEQUENCE

Bill Clinton opened the door. Standing there were Kerry and Biden, big grins on their face. "God love ya, Bill, you look like shit."

"Hello, dear."

"Have you ever been to Siberia?"

"I'll get a coat."

ABOUT THE AUTHOR

Oliver Willis was one of the first political bloggers in the world and has been writing at OliverWillis.com since 2001. He writes about politics and can be seen daily @owillis. He lives in Takoma Park, Maryland.

Made in the USA
Lexington, KY
26 January 2018